MARGRET & H. A. REY'S

Curious George Goes to the Zoo

Written by Cynthia Platt

Illustrated in the style of H. A. Rey by Mary O'Keefe Young

HOUGHTON MIFFLIN HARCOURT

Boston New York

To Dad, and trips to San Diego
—C.P.

For Bridget, my inspiration
—M.O'K.Y.

www.hmhco.com

The text of this book was set in Adobe Garamond.
The illustrations are watercolor.

ISBN 978-0-544-11000-7

Manufactured in China
SCP 10 9 8 7 6 5 4 3

4500526952

This is George. George is a good little monkey and always very curious. Today, George was feeling very excited. The man with the yellow hat was taking him to the zoo!

As they drove, the man explained to George that this wasn't just any zoo that they were going to visit.

"It's called the Wild Animal Park," the man said. "All of the animals roam around freely."

When they arrived, George saw a huge banner. George looked up at it, but he could not read the words.

A friendly zookeeper explained.

“It’s an extra-special day here at the Wild Animal Park,” she said. “It is our baby rhino’s first birthday. We are going to have a party for her later on!”

A party! This was going to be a wonderful trip to the zoo.

George tried to walk
into the park where the
animals were, but the
zookeeper stopped him.

"You can't walk in there!" she said.

"To explore this zoo, you have to ride in one of our special cars."

She pointed to a huge car that had no roof on it.

Oh, my! What fun this was going to be.

George and his friend climbed onboard and the car drove into the park.

Soon they were in the midst of the Wild Animal Park.

"Look over there!" said the zookeeper. "There's our pride of lions. We have a large family here."

George pointed in the other direction. "Yes, George," said the zookeeper. "I see the giraffes, too. Their tall necks help them eat leaves from the treetops. And there are two ostriches running this way!"

George was happy to be seeing so many amazing animals.

The zoo car drove past a small pond. Pink flamingos waded in the water. Their heads bobbed up and down as they walked on spindly legs.

"The flamingos turn pink because they eat so many tiny pink shrimp," said the zoo-keeper, but George was not listening.

He had never seen flamingos before. He was curious about how those flamingos were moving.

He leaned out the back of the zoo car as far as he could to take a look. But then—oh! What happened?

First George lost his balance. Then he fell—*kerplunk!*—right out of the zoo car. His friend hadn't noticed that he had fallen. George ran as quickly as a little monkey could toward the pond.

The flamingos bobbed their heads and lifted their feet one at a time. It looked like they were dancing. George danced with them.

Suddenly, the water in the pond started to move. Then a hippo popped its head out from under the water. What a surprise! George stopped dancing to take a look.

The hippo opened its huge mouth as if it were yawning. George opened his mouth wide, too. It was fun to act like the hippo!

Just then, George noticed that something was rustling in the reeds near the pond. George was curious. He wanted to see what was there.

In an instant, he jumped over to the reeds. He poked his nose inside and saw . . . a baby rhino!

The tiny rhino was cute, but she looked a little bit sad and a little bit lonely.

George wanted to make that baby rhino feel happy again. He thought and thought. Maybe the baby rhino would like the flamingo dance.

He jumped and bobbed his head and danced his feet up and down.

The baby rhino peeked her head out of the reeds so that she could watch. George danced more, and the rhino walked out of the reeds.

She was curious, too!

They were having so much fun that George didn't notice what was behind him.

The zookeeper stomped over to George. She did not look happy. The man with the yellow hat was running behind her.

"You are a naughty little monkey," said the zookeeper. "You were supposed to stay in the car. You and your friend will have to go now."

George walked to the man's side. He waved goodbye to the baby rhino. The man and the zookeeper turned to see whom George was waving to.

"The baby rhino! Why, we've been looking for her all day," said the zookeeper. "She got separated from her mother."

George was glad to see the zookeeper looking happy again. He and the man started walking toward the exit.

The zookeeper ran to stop them. "Thank you for finding our baby rhino, George. And just in time for her birthday party. Will you join us for some cake?"

George jumped with glee. He had forgotten about the party, and he did love cake.

The man and George followed the zookeeper and the baby rhino back to zoo headquarters. The rhino's mother was waiting there for her.

The zookeeper brought out a special birthday cake that was shaped like a rhino. George had never seen a cake like that before.

"You can have the first piece, George," said the zookeeper. "I also have a special treat, just for you!" She placed a bunch of bananas in front of him.

George was very happy to have a tasty banana, but he saved room for some cake, too!